How to Build the Best Fort Ever:

A Fun Guide to Creating Awesome Indoor and Outdoor Forts with Blankets, Pillows, and Natural Materials

Ashton Gunnell & Colleen Cummings

Table of Contents

Chapter 6: Themed Forts: Adventure Awaits

- Pirate Ship Fort
- Jungle Safari Fort
- Princess Castle or Superhero Hideout

Chapter 7: Fort Safety: Keeping Fun Safe

- Indoor Safety
- Outdoor Safety
- Weather Considerations

Chapter 8: Games and Activities Inside Your Fort

- Imagination Games
- Movie Night in Your Fort
- Fort Challenges

Chapter 9: Fort Sleepovers and Picnics: Making It an Event

- Overnight Fort Adventures
- Fort Picnics
- Fort Campfires (Indoor Version)

Chapter 10: Taking Down and Rebuilding: The Fun Continues

- How to Safely Dismantle Your Fort
- The Joy of Rebuilding
- Encouraging Teamwork

Conclusion: Keep Building Adventures!

Introduction: Welcome to the World of Forts!

Welcome to the most amazing book about forts ever! My name is Ashton, and I'm super excited to take you on this fun journey into the world of fort building. Have you ever wanted to escape to a magical land, become a pirate captain, or just have the coolest hangout spot with your friends? Well, building a fort is the perfect way to do all of that!

Forts are not just piles of blankets and cushions—they're adventures waiting to happen! When you build a fort, you're not just creating a cozy space; you're unleashing your imagination and creativity. Whether it's a blanket fort in your living room or a natural fort made of sticks and leaves outside, each fort has its own story to tell.

In this book, you'll learn all about the magic of fort building. We'll explore different types of forts, what supplies you'll need, and how to design your very own cozy hideaway. Plus, I'll share tons of fun activities, games, and ideas to make your fort the best place ever!

You'll find step-by-step guides to help you build your fort, whether it's a classic blanket fort or a wild jungle hideout. You'll discover how to plan awesome sleepovers and picnics, and even how to host your very own Fort Olympics with your friends!

So grab your pillows, blankets, and all your favorite supplies, and get ready for an exciting adventure. Let's build some incredible forts and make amazing memories together. The world of forts is waiting for you—let's dive in and start creating!

Happy fort building!

Ashton

Chapter 1: The Magic of Fort Building

Hey, Fort Builders!

Guess what? Today, we're going on an adventure. And no, not the kind where you need a map and a backpack (well, unless you want to). We're going on an adventure **right at home** or maybe in your backyard! We're going to talk about one of the coolest things ever: **building forts**!

Do you like building stuff with LEGOs? Or maybe you've built a sandcastle at the beach before? Well, building a fort is kind of like that but **way more fun** because you get to use blankets, pillows, sticks, chairs… anything! It's like being an architect (that's a fancy word for people who design buildings) but in a much cooler way because it's YOUR fort, and you're in charge of making it awesome.

Let me tell you why fort building is the BEST thing ever.

Why Build a Fort? Forts Are Like Magic!

Ever think about why forts are so amazing? It's because forts are like **a portal to another world**. Once you crawl inside, it's like you're in a **whole new place**. One minute you're in your living room, and the next—BOOM—you're the captain of a pirate ship sailing the seven seas, or a jungle explorer hunting for treasure, or maybe you're a queen or king in your castle ruling the land!

Here's why forts are super cool:

- **You Can Be Anything You Want!** When you build a fort, you can pretend to be anything. You could be hiding out from dragons, setting up a camp in the jungle, or even running a secret spy mission. Your fort is like a **stage** where you get to play out whatever's in your imagination!
- **You Get to Make the Rules.** Want your fort to have a lookout tower? Cool, you can do that. Want a secret door that only YOU know how to open? Totally possible. Want to have the coziest space with 10 pillows and string lights? Go for it! Your fort, your rules.
- **You Get Super Creative!** Building forts is like building with LEGOs but way bigger. You get to figure out how to make everything fit together. How can you make a roof that stays up? How do you make a comfy floor? It's like solving a fun puzzle, but with stuff from around the house or outside.

The Epic Showdown: Indoor vs. Outdoor Forts

Let's talk about the two types of forts. They're both awesome, but they're a little different.

Indoor Forts: Cozy & Secret

Indoor forts are the coziest things ever. Imagine this: it's raining outside, you've got your favorite blanket, and you're ready to build the **best fort ever** in the living room. You can grab some chairs, a bunch of blankets, and all the pillows you can find! You can even steal (um, I mean borrow) your parents' couch cushions. The best part? Once it's built, it's like a super secret hideout right in your house. You can bring in snacks, books, and maybe even your tablet if you want to have a movie night in there.

Why I love indoor forts:

One time, I built an indoor fort with my little sister, and we made a "no adults allowed" sign. We had popcorn, flashlights, and even played cards inside. It was like our own little clubhouse, and no one could come in without the secret password. Indoor forts are great for being comfy and sneaky at the same time.

Outdoor Forts: Wild & Adventurous

Outdoor forts are a whole different kind of awesome. Imagine being outside, with the wind blowing, and you're building a fort with **real sticks** and **leaves**. It's like you're an adventurer out in the wild, building a shelter to survive. You can find long branches to make the walls, use big rocks to hold everything down, and maybe even use a tarp to make sure rain doesn't get in.

Why I love outdoor forts:

One summer, I built an outdoor fort with my cousins in the backyard. We pretended it was a pirate camp, and we used leaves and branches to camouflage it so nobody could find us. We even made a lookout tower by climbing up the tree next to it. The coolest part? We stayed outside in the fort until it got dark, and we used flashlights to make shadow puppets on the fort walls. Outside forts make me feel like I'm on a real adventure, surviving in the wild!

Forts Let You Be Creative

When you build a fort, you get to be creative in so many ways. You get to think about how you want to build it, what you want to decorate it with, and how you want to use it. Here are some of the most fun things about being creative with forts:

- **Decoration Fun**: You can decorate your fort with anything! Maybe you want to use your favorite blanket or add some stuffed animals to guard the entrance. You can even add cool lights like fairy lights or glow sticks to make it feel magical inside.
- **Secret Spaces**: Every fort needs a secret room, right? Maybe you have a secret entrance only you know about, or a hidden spot where you can stash snacks or toys. Adding secret spaces makes your fort feel like a real hideout.

- **Themes**: You can build a different fort every time. One day, you might build a jungle fort, and the next day, it's a spaceship! You can change the theme by adding decorations that match what you're pretending.

Let's Do Something Fun! First Fort Activity!

Okay, now that you know how awesome fort building is, let's get started with a fun activity. This is going to help you plan your **dream fort**.

Activity 1: Design Your Dream Fort!
Grab some paper and crayons or markers. We're going to draw out what your dream fort would look like! You can be as creative as you want. Here are some ideas to think about while you draw:

1. **Where will you build it?** Will it be inside with blankets and pillows? Or will you build it outside with sticks and leaves?
2. **What will it look like?** Is it big and tall, or small and cozy? Will it have windows, secret doors, or a lookout tower?
3. **How many rooms will it have?** Maybe it has one big room for hanging out, or maybe it has different rooms for different activities.
4. **What's the theme?** Is it a pirate ship, a castle, a jungle camp, or maybe even a space station?

Once you're done drawing, you'll have the blueprints for your ultimate fort! This will help you plan out your building process when you're ready to get started. Plus, it's super fun to think about all the cool things you can do with your fort!

How Building Forts Helps You Team Up

Building forts isn't just about **you**. It's even more fun when you team up with your friends, your siblings, or even your parents (if they're cool enough to help). When you work together, you can make your fort even bigger and better. Here's why teamwork is super important in fort building:

- **More Ideas**: When you work with other people, they might have ideas that you never even thought about! Maybe your friend has an idea for a super cool secret tunnel, or your brother knows how to make the roof stand up better.
- **Bigger Forts**: With more people helping, you can build forts that are way bigger than you could do on your own. Imagine a fort that stretches across the whole living room or a backyard fort with multiple rooms!
- **More Fun**: Building forts with others is just more fun! You can laugh together, solve problems, and celebrate when you finish the fort.

Indoor vs. Outdoor: Which Fort Is Better?

So now you know about indoor and outdoor forts. But which one is better? Well, that's up to you! Here's a little side-by-side comparison to help you decide which one you want to try building first.

Indoor Forts	Outdoor Forts
Cozy and warm	Wild and adventurous
Easy to build with blankets	Use real sticks and leaves
Great for rainy days	Perfect for sunny days
Safe and comfy	Feels like a real explorer camp

Both are super fun, and you don't have to pick just one. You can build an indoor fort today and an outdoor fort tomorrow!

Bonus Fort Ideas!

Before we finish this chapter, here are some **bonus fort ideas** to get your imagination going:

- **Animal Fort**: Pretend you're an animal in the jungle or the forest. Build your fort like a nest or a den, and fill it with stuffed animals!
- **Space Fort**: Use blankets and pillows to create a space station. Hang some glow-in-the-dark stars and pretend you're floating through space.
- **Campground Fort**: Build a fort that looks like a tent, and pretend you're camping in the wilderness. Bring snacks like marshmallows and tell ghost stories inside!

Okay, Fort Builders, are you ready to start your fort-building adventure? In the next chapter, we'll talk about all the cool stuff you need to gather before you start building. But for now,

Here's the draft for Chapter 2, written in the same playful style to keep the kids engaged, while hitting the target length of 2,500 words:

Chapter 2: Fort Fundamentals – What You'll Need

Hey, Fort Masters!

Before we dive into building your super cool fort, we need to make sure you have **all the right stuff**. Just like when you go on a treasure hunt and need a map, a compass, and maybe even a sword (because pirates, obviously!), you need the right tools and materials to build your fort. Don't worry, though—we're not talking about hammers and nails. We're talking about fun stuff like blankets, pillows, and sticks!

Let's start by making a list of everything you'll need for the **ultimate fort-building session**. There are different supplies for indoor and outdoor forts, so I'll cover both, plus a few secret tips to make your fort **extra awesome**.

Indoor Fort Essentials: Cozy and Creative

Building an indoor fort is like creating the coziest, coolest space ever. Imagine crawling into your fort and feeling all snuggly with your blankets, pillows, and maybe even some twinkly lights! But first, we need to gather our supplies.

Here's what you'll need for building your epic indoor fort:

1. **Blankets (Lots and Lots of Blankets!)**
   Blankets are the key to building your fort's walls and roof. The bigger and softer, the

better! Ask your parents if you can use the couch blankets, bed sheets, or even sleeping bags. You can also mix and match different types of blankets to make your fort colorful and unique.

Pro Tip: Don't forget to ask permission before raiding the linen closet. Trust me, you don't want to accidentally use your mom's fancy quilt!

2. **Pillows (Fort Builders Need Comfort)**

   Pillows aren't just for sleeping—they're for **making forts cozy**. Grab all the pillows you can find! You can use them to make a soft floor inside your fort, or you can pile them up to create walls or a comfy seating area.

   Bonus Idea: Try stacking pillows to make a secret wall or even a little tunnel that leads into your fort!

3. **Chairs, Sofas, and Furniture**

   To build a strong fort, you'll need something to hold up the blankets. Chairs are perfect for this! Place a couple of chairs back-to-back and drape a blanket over them to make the roof of your fort. You can also use the back of the sofa or the coffee table to help support the walls.

   Extra Cool Tip: If you use different heights of furniture (like tall chairs and low tables), you can create different "rooms" in your fort!

4. **Clips, Rubber Bands, or Clothes Pins**

   Sometimes, blankets can slip off chairs or fall down when you're in the middle of a fort-building marathon. That's where clips come in! Use **clothespins** or **rubber bands** to keep the blankets in place. Trust me, this little trick will keep your fort from collapsing halfway through movie night!

5. **Lights!**

   No fort is complete without some **cool lighting**. You can use flashlights, lanterns, or even string lights to make your fort feel magical. Just imagine how cozy it'll be to crawl into your fort and turn on a string of fairy lights!

   Warning: Don't use real candles or anything with an open flame. Forts are made of fabric, and fire is a big no-no!

6. **Snacks and Drinks**

   Okay, this isn't technically part of the fort structure, but **you'll need snacks** to survive inside your fort for long adventures. Pack some popcorn, chips, or your favorite candy, and don't forget a drink. Building forts is hard work!

7. **Toys and Books**

   Once your fort is built, you'll want to fill it with fun stuff! Bring in some of your favorite toys, stuffed animals, or books. Whether you're reading stories or having an action figure battle, having some entertainment inside your fort is key to having the best time ever.

Outdoor Fort Essentials: Adventure Awaits

Building an outdoor fort is like being a **real explorer**. You get to use things from nature, like sticks and leaves, and create a hidden hideout right in your backyard or in a park. The great thing about outdoor forts is that you can make them as big as you want, and you get to use **natural materials**.

Here's what you'll need to get started on your outdoor adventure fort:

1. **Sticks, Branches, and Logs**
   Sticks are the main building blocks for outdoor forts. You'll need sturdy branches to make the frame of your fort. Look around your yard or nearby woods for sticks that are long and thick. The best branches are the ones that are straight and strong enough to hold up your fort's roof.
   Safety Tip: Be careful when you pick up branches. Don't choose ones that are too heavy or have sharp edges. You can also ask an adult to help you find the best ones.

2. **Rocks (Nature's Building Blocks)**
   Rocks can help hold things down, like tarps or sticks that need extra weight. They can also be used to make a cool entrance path or outline the "rooms" inside your fort. Just look around and see if you can find some smooth, flat rocks that are easy to carry.
   Cool Idea: Use rocks to build a little "fire pit" outside your fort. You won't light a real fire, but it's fun to pretend you have a campfire for telling stories at night.

3. **Tarps or Blankets**
   If you want your outdoor fort to be **waterproof**, you'll need a tarp. Tarps are great for keeping out the rain or wind. If you don't have a tarp, you can also use an old blanket or sheet to create a roof for your outdoor fort. Just make sure it's something you don't mind getting a little dirty!
   Pro Tip: Use ropes or rubber bands to tie the tarp or blanket to trees or branches. This will help keep it from blowing away in the wind.

4. **Ropes and String**
   Ropes are super handy for building outdoor forts. You can use them to tie sticks together to make walls, or you can string them between trees to hold up the roof. If you don't have a rope, string or twine will work just as well.
   Safety Tip: Make sure the ropes are tied tightly so your fort doesn't fall apart. Also, be careful not to trip over any loose ends!

5. **Leaves and Grass**
   Want to make your fort look like it's hidden in the jungle? Use **leaves and grass** to cover the outside of your fort. You can pile them on top of your fort to camouflage it so that no one can find you! Plus, they're soft and can make a comfy floor for your fort.
   Bonus Idea: Try weaving some tall grass or leaves together to make a natural "door" for your fort.

Organizing Your Supplies: Get Ready to Build!

Now that you know what you need, it's time to **get organized**. This is an important step because you don't want to start building and then realize you forgot something. Trust me, it's no fun to run inside to grab a pillow when you're already halfway through building the best fort ever.

Here's how to get organized before you start:

1. **Make a Supply Pile**
   Before you start building, gather all your supplies in one spot. Whether you're building

inside or outside, make a pile of everything you'll need—blankets, pillows, sticks, chairs, rocks, snacks, lights, and anything else. This way, everything will be close by, and you won't have to stop building to find more materials.

2. **Check the Weather (If You're Outside)**
   If you're building an outdoor fort, you'll want to check the weather. If it's sunny and dry, you're good to go! But if it's raining or super windy, you might want to wait for a better day. Forts are more fun when you're not soaking wet or battling the wind!

3. **Ask for Help (If You Need It)**
   Building a fort can be a big job, especially if you're making a giant one! Don't be afraid to ask for help from a sibling, friend, or even your parents. They can help hold up the blankets or tie the ropes, and together, you'll build an even cooler fort.

4. **Think About the Space**
   Whether you're building indoors or outdoors, think about where your fort will go. Make sure there's enough room for you to build your masterpiece! If you're inside, check that you're not blocking any doors or walking paths. If you're outside, choose a flat area that's free of sharp

objects like rocks or branches that might make the ground uncomfortable or unsafe.

5. **Make a Fort Plan**
   Just like a real builder, it helps to have a plan before you start. Do you want your fort to have one big room or several smaller rooms? Will it have a secret entrance? Will there be a lookout post? Think about how you want your fort to look and where everything will go. Drawing a quick sketch or talking through your ideas with your team (if you have one) can make things easier when it's time to build.

Let's Get Ready to Build!

Now that you've gathered everything you need and organized your supplies, you're ready to start building! But wait! Before we dive into construction, I have a fun little activity to get you even more excited about fort building.

Activity: Fort Builders' Supply Check!

This activity will help you make sure you've got all the essentials for your fort. You can also add your own special items to the list. Ready? Let's go!

Instructions:

1. Grab a piece of paper and a pencil.
2. Write down all the things you want to use in your fort. Start with the basics like blankets, pillows, chairs, sticks, and ropes.
3. Now, think about any **special items** you want to include. Maybe you want to add your favorite stuffed animal, a flashlight, or a snack stash! Write those down too.
4. Check off each item as you gather them. Once everything is checked off, you're officially ready to build your fort!

Example List:

- Blankets
- Pillows
- Chairs (for holding up blankets)
- Flashlight
- Snacks (lots of snacks!)
- Favorite book
- Rope (for outdoor forts)

Feel free to add as many items as you want! This is your fort, so don't be afraid to get creative with your supplies.

Bonus: Super Secret Fort Supply Tips

Now that you know the basics, here are some **extra tips** to take your fort to the next level!

1. **Use Heavy Blankets for the Roof**
   If you're building an indoor fort, use heavier blankets like comforters or quilts for the roof. These will help block out light and make the inside of your fort feel extra cozy and dark—perfect for movie nights or telling ghost stories!
2. **Create a Super Soft Floor**
   If you want to be really comfy inside your fort, pile up pillows and blankets on the floor. You can even bring in a sleeping bag or mattress pad if you're planning to have a sleepover inside your fort.
3. **Add a Fort "Flag"**
   Want to claim your fort as your own? Make a fort flag! Grab an old piece of fabric or paper, draw a symbol on it (like a pirate skull or a castle emblem), and hang it on the outside of your fort to show everyone that **this fort belongs to you**.
4. **Camouflage Your Outdoor Fort**
   If you're building a fort outside and you want it to be **super secret**, cover it with leaves, branches, and grass to make it blend in with nature. This will help hide it from anyone who might be snooping around!
5. **Bring a Book or Journal**
   Once your fort is built, it's fun to have a little alone time inside. Bring a book, comic, or

even a journal, and spend some quiet time reading or writing in your fort. It's like having your own little hideaway where you can relax and let your imagination run wild.

Wrapping Up: What's Next?

Wow, we've covered a lot in this chapter, haven't we? Now you know exactly what you'll need to build your fort, whether you're indoors or outdoors. You've got your supplies list, your plan, and some extra tips to make your fort the best it can be.

In the next chapter, we're going to dive into actually **building your fort**. I'll show you step-by-step instructions on how to make the **coziest indoor fort** and the **most adventurous outdoor fort** ever. But for now, make sure you've got everything ready and maybe start thinking about where you'll build your fort.

Pro Tip: Try practicing setting up a mini-fort with just a few items. This will get you even more pumped up for the real deal!

So, are you ready to build the **ultimate fort**? Let's get those supplies organized, and I'll meet you in the next chapter where we'll start the **construction phase** of your fort-building adventure!

Chapter 3: Indoor Fort Designs: Cozy & Creative

Hey there, Fort Experts!

Now that you've got all your supplies ready, it's time to get down to the really fun part—**building your indoor fort**! Whether you want a cozy little hideout to curl up in with a book, or you're planning a massive fort with secret rooms and tunnels, I've got you covered.

We're going to start by talking about some of the best **indoor fort designs**. Trust me, after this chapter, you'll be a fort-building master. So grab your blankets, pillows, and let's dive in!

The Classic Blanket Fort: Old School, But Always Awesome

Let's start with the classic—the one and only **blanket fort**. You know the one. You drape blankets over chairs, pull out some pillows, and BAM—you've got yourself a cozy hideaway. Even though it's a simple design, there are lots of ways to make it super cool.

How to Build a Classic Blanket Fort:

1. **Step 1: Gather Your Building Materials**
   You'll need chairs, blankets, pillows, and maybe some clothespins or rubber bands to hold everything in place. If you want your fort to be extra sturdy, try using heavy blankets or bedspreads for the roof.
2. **Step 2: Set Up the Chairs**
   Put two or three chairs back-to-back. The taller the chairs, the higher your fort roof will be. Leave some space between the chairs so you can crawl in and out easily.
   Pro Tip: Try to use chairs with tall backs so your fort feels roomy inside. If your chairs are short, your fort might feel a little squished.
3. **Step 3: Drape the Blankets**
   Take your biggest blankets and drape them over the top of the chairs. Let the sides of the blankets hang down so they touch the floor. This will create your fort walls. You can tuck the blanket ends under the chairs to keep them from falling off.
   Bonus Idea: If you want windows, leave a small gap between two blankets to peek out of!
4. **Step 4: Add Pillows and Cushions**
   Now it's time to get cozy! Pile up pillows and cushions inside the fort to make a comfy floor. You can even add stuffed animals or a sleeping bag if you're planning on hanging out for a long time.
5. **Step 5: Lights and Decorations**
   This is the fun part—adding your **personal touch**! Bring in a flashlight, some fairy lights, or even a little lantern to light up the inside. You can also decorate with your favorite stuffed animals, posters, or drawings.

And just like that, you've got a classic blanket fort! This type of fort is perfect for reading, playing games, or just chilling out. It's super easy to build and doesn't take long to set up.

Theme Forts: Take Your Fort to the Next Level

Now that you know how to build the classic fort, let's talk about **themed forts**. This is where you can really let your imagination go wild! Instead of just building a regular fort, you can turn it into a whole new world—a castle, a spaceship, a secret hideout, or even a pirate ship.

Here are some fun ideas for themed forts:

1. **The Castle Fort**
   Pretend you're a king or queen ruling over your kingdom! Use tall chairs to make high walls, and drape blankets over the top to create towers. You can even add a drawbridge by laying a blanket across the entrance and pulling it up when you don't want any "intruders" coming inside.
   Extra Cool Tip: Make a crown out of paper or tinfoil to wear while you're in your castle fort!
2. **The Spaceship Fort**
   Blast off into space with your very own **spaceship fort**! Use shiny silver blankets or sheets (if you have them) to make your fort look like a spaceship. You can add cardboard tubes or paper towel rolls as "rocket boosters" on the outside. Inside, bring in your tablet or a pretend control panel and imagine you're flying through space.
   Bonus Idea: Cut out some stars from paper and hang them inside your fort to make it feel like you're floating in space!
3. **The Secret Spy Fort**
   Every good spy needs a **secret base**. Build a hidden fort in the corner of the room, using blankets and pillows to make a small but sneaky hideout. Add a secret entrance by hanging a blanket over the doorway that only you know how to get through. You can even make a "spy kit" with a flashlight, notebook, and invisible ink pens to plan your missions.
   Spy Mission: Write down secret messages and store them inside your spy fort. Don't let anyone find them!

Lighting and Comfort: How to Make Your Fort Super Cozy

Once you've built your fort, it's time to make it **super cozy**! The inside of your fort is your special space, and you want it to feel comfy and magical. Here are some ideas for how to make your fort the best hangout spot ever:

1. **Twinkling Lights**
   Want your fort to feel like a fairy tale? Add some **twinkling lights**! You can use string lights, Christmas lights, or even glow-in-the-dark stars to light up your fort. Hang them on the inside walls or along the roof to create a magical glow.
   Pro Tip: If you don't have string lights, you can make your fort glow with flashlights or glow sticks. They're just as fun!
2. **Comfy Pillows and Blankets**
   Pile up as many pillows as you can find! The floor of your fort should be super soft so you can lay down and relax. You can also bring in your favorite blanket or sleeping bag to make it extra cozy. If you want, throw in a few stuffed animals to keep you company.
3. **Mini TV Room**
   Ever wanted your own private movie theater? Turn your fort into a **mini TV room**! Bring in a tablet or phone and set up a cozy spot where you can watch your favorite shows or movies. You can even make some popcorn and pretend you're at the movies.
   Bonus Tip: Make a "movie night" sign to hang on the front of your fort. Invite your friends or family to join you for a fort movie night!
4. **Snack Station**
   Every great fort needs snacks! Set up a small corner of your fort as a **snack station**. You can bring in chips, cookies, or even sandwiches if you're planning to stay inside for a while. Don't forget to bring a drink (but be careful not to spill)!

Secret Fort Features: Make Your Fort Extra Cool

Now that you've built your fort and made it cozy, let's add some secret features to make it even cooler. These little tricks will make your fort feel like a real adventure!

1. **Secret Doorway**
   Every good fort needs a secret entrance! You can make a secret door by leaving one side of the fort open just a little, then covering it with a blanket. Only you will know where the entrance is, and you can sneak in and out without anyone seeing you!
   Cool Idea: Make a password for anyone who wants to come into your fort. If they don't know the password, they can't get in!
2. **Hidden Treasure Chest**
   If you're building a pirate fort or a castle, you'll need a place to hide your treasure! Find a small box or container and put it inside your fort. You can fill it with candy, toys, or secret notes. Hide it under a blanket or in the corner of your fort, so no one finds your loot.
   Treasure Hunt Game: Invite your friends to search for the hidden treasure inside your fort. The first one to find it wins a prize!
3. **Escape Tunnel**
   Want to make your fort feel like a real hideout? Build an **escape tunnel**! All you need is a long blanket or sheet that you can crawl under to escape the fort. Place it behind your chairs or couch, and it'll lead out of the fort like a secret tunnel.

Adventure Idea: Pretend you're escaping from dragons, pirates, or enemy spies by crawling through your escape tunnel!

Activity: Fort Challenge – Design Your Ultimate Theme Fort

Now it's time for a fun fort-building challenge! I want you to design your very own **theme fort**. Here's what you need to do:

1. **Pick a Theme**
   Will your fort be a pirate ship, a jungle safari hideout, or maybe even a superhero base? Choose a theme that sounds fun to you.
2. **Draw Your Fort**
   Grab some paper and crayons or markers. Draw a picture of your fort and label all the cool features. Do you have a lookout tower? A secret entrance? A treasure chest? Make sure to include those in your drawing.
3. **Build Your Fort**
   Once your design is finished, it's time to build! Use all the ideas from this chapter to create the most epic themed fort ever.
4. **Show Off Your Fort**
   Invite your family or friends to check out your fort. Give them a tour and show off all the awesome features you included.

Wrapping Up: Let the Fort Adventures Begin!

By now, you're practically a **fort-building pro**. You know how to build the classic blanket fort, create themed forts, and add secret features to make them even more fun. The best part? Every fort is different, and you can build a new one every time you play!

In the next chapter, we'll talk about **outdoor forts** and how to build awesome hideouts using nature. But for now, go grab some blankets, build your indoor fort, and let your imagination take over. Whether you're ruling a kingdom, flying through space, or going on a secret spy mission, your fort is your personal adventure world!

Chapter 4: Outdoor Forts: Embrace Nature

Hey Fort Explorers!

Guess what? We're taking our fort-building skills **outside**! Yup, it's time to get out into the wild, grab some sticks, leaves, and rocks, and build a fort that would make any adventurer proud. Outdoor forts are totally different from indoor forts because instead of blankets and pillows, we get to use nature's materials like branches, grass, and stones.

Building an outdoor fort feels like a real adventure. It's like you're out in the wild, building a shelter to survive! Are you ready? Let's get our outdoor gear on and start exploring how to make the **best outdoor fort ever**!

Nature's Materials: Build with What You Find

Building an outdoor fort means using all the cool things nature gives us. Look around your backyard, a park, or a forest, and you'll find **tons of awesome materials** you can use to make your fort. The great thing about outdoor forts is that they blend in with nature, and sometimes, they can even be **camouflaged**!

Here's a list of some things you can use to build your outdoor fort:

1. **Sticks and Branches**
   Sticks are the best for building your fort's frame. Find sturdy, long branches to use as the walls and roof of your fort. You can lean them against each other or tie them together with rope or string to create a strong structure.
   Pro Tip: Try to find branches that are as tall as you! This will make sure your fort has high enough walls so you can stand (or at least kneel) inside.
2. **Leaves and Grass**
   Once you have your structure, you can use leaves and grass to cover the outside of your fort. This will make your fort feel more like a real hideout. Plus, if you use a lot of leaves, it'll blend in with the surroundings so no one can see it from far away!
   Bonus Idea: Use leaves to create a **soft floor** inside your fort. Just pile them up so you can sit or lay down on a comfy leaf bed.
3. **Rocks**
   Big rocks can help hold down any tarps or blankets you might use, and they're also great for making the base of your fort stronger. You can line the outside of your fort with rocks to make it sturdy and windproof.
   Cool Idea: Build a pretend **fire pit** outside your fort using rocks. You won't light a real fire, but it's fun to sit around the "campfire" and tell stories!
4. **Ropes or String**
   If you have rope or string, you can use it to tie sticks together to make a stronger frame. You can also tie a tarp or blanket to trees using the rope to create a waterproof roof for

your fort.

Safety Tip: Make sure you don't tie the ropes too tightly around the trees or branches—you want them to hold the fort up, but not hurt the trees!

Teepee or Lean-To Forts: Simple but Sturdy

When it comes to building outdoor forts, there are two really awesome types of structures you can try: the **teepee** and the **lean-to**. Both of these forts are easy to build, and they're perfect for using natural materials like sticks and leaves.

How to Build a Teepee Fort

A **teepee** is shaped like a cone, with sticks leaning together to make a cozy, round space inside. Here's how you can build your very own teepee fort:

1. **Step 1: Find the Perfect Spot**
   Look for a nice, flat area in your yard or in a park. Make sure there's enough space for your teepee to stand without falling over. It helps if you have some trees nearby to lean the sticks against.

2. **Step 2: Gather Long Sticks**
    You'll need **at least six long sticks** that are sturdy enough to stand up straight. The taller the sticks, the bigger your teepee will be! You can also use more than six sticks if you want a bigger fort.
3. **Step 3: Set Up the Frame**
    Place one end of each stick on the ground and lean the tops of the sticks together in the center. It's okay if they crisscross a little—this is what holds the sticks together! Make sure the space between the sticks is wide enough for you to crawl inside.
    Pro Tip: If you have some rope or string, you can tie the tops of the sticks together to make the frame more secure.
4. **Step 4: Cover with Leaves or Grass**
    Once your frame is set up, it's time to cover it! Find big leaves, grass, or even pine branches to place around the outside of your teepee. This will give your fort walls and help keep the inside cool and shady.
5. **Step 5: Add the Finishing Touches**
    Now that your teepee is built, add some finishing touches! Pile up leaves inside to make a soft floor, or use rocks to decorate the outside. You can even hang some string or ribbon from the top of the teepee to make it feel like a real adventure fort!

How to Build a Lean-To Fort

A **lean-to** fort is like a mini house that leans against something, like a tree or a fence. It's super easy to build and is great for hiding out on a sunny day.

1. **Step 1: Find Something to Lean Against**
    Look for a tall tree, a fence, or even a wall to build your fort against. This will be the "back" of your fort.
2. **Step 2: Collect Long Sticks**
    Just like the teepee, you'll need long sticks for the frame. The sticks will lean against the tree or fence to create the walls and roof.
3. **Step 3: Set Up the Sticks**
    Place one end of each stick on the ground, and lean the other end against the tree or fence. Make sure the sticks are spaced evenly so they don't fall over.
    Pro Tip: You can use some string or rope to tie the sticks together at the top to make sure they stay in place.
4. **Step 4: Cover with Leaves, Grass, or a Tarp**
    Now, cover the sticks with leaves, grass, or a tarp if you have one. This will create the roof and walls of your fort. Make sure to cover any gaps so no sunlight (or rain) can get through.

5. **Step 5: Decorate and Play!**
   Once your lean-to is ready, decorate it with some rocks, leaves, or even wildflowers. Then, crawl inside and enjoy your awesome outdoor fort!

Weatherproofing Your Fort: Stay Dry and Warm

One of the cool things about outdoor forts is that you get to deal with the **weather**! Whether it's sunny, rainy, or windy, your fort can handle it if you know how to **weatherproof** it.

Here are some tips to keep your fort safe from the weather:

1. **Rainy Day Ready**
   If it looks like rain, cover your fort with a tarp, plastic sheet, or even an old blanket to keep the water out. Make sure to weigh down the edges with rocks so the wind doesn't blow the cover away.
   Cool Idea: Dig a small trench around the outside of your fort to help water drain away from it. This will keep the inside of your fort dry!
2. **Wind-Proof Your Fort**
   On a windy day, use rocks or heavy logs to hold down the edges of your fort. You can also build your fort next to a tree or large bush to block the wind.
   Bonus Tip: Lean your sticks against a solid structure, like a tree or fence, to make sure they don't blow away.
3. **Sunny Days**
   On a hot, sunny day, use leaves and branches to cover your fort and create shade. The thicker the walls, the cooler it'll be inside!

Bonus Fort Challenge: Outdoor Fort Obstacle Course

Here's a fun challenge to try once you've built your outdoor fort! Create an **obstacle course** that leads to your fort. This will make it feel like you're on a real adventure!

1. **Create a Path**
   Use rocks, sticks, or chalk to make a path leading to your fort. You can add "traps" along the way, like stepping stones or a log to jump over.
2. **Add Challenges**
   Make your path more exciting by adding challenges like crawling under a low-hanging branch, balancing on a log, or hopping from rock to rock without touching the ground.
3. **Time It**
   Challenge your friends or family to race through the obstacle course. The fastest person to make it through and reach the fort wins!

Wrapping Up: Your Outdoor Adventure Awaits!

Building an outdoor fort is an adventure like no other. You get to use the materials you find in nature, work with trees and sticks, and create something totally unique. Plus, the fresh air makes it even more fun! Whether you build a teepee, a lean-to, or something completely new, your outdoor fort will be your **ultimate hideout**.

In the next chapter, we're going to take fort building to the next level by adding **multiple rooms** and **secret spaces**! But for now, get outside, find the perfect spot, and start building your amazing outdoor fort.

Fun Outdoor Activities to Enjoy Inside Your Fort

Now that you've built your awesome outdoor fort, it's time to make it even more fun! Once you're inside your fort, there are tons of exciting activities you can do. Here are some ideas to keep you entertained and make the most of your new hideaway:

1. **Nature Scavenger Hunt**
   Turn your fort area into a scavenger hunt zone! Before you head into your fort, create a list of things to find in nature, like different types of leaves, flowers, rocks, or bugs. Once you've gathered everything, head back to your fort to show off your treasures!
   Sample Scavenger Hunt List:
   - A smooth rock
   - A leaf with five points
   - A flower (any color!)
   - Something that makes noise (like a bug or rustling leaves)
   - A stick shaped like a letter (A, B, C, etc.)
2. **Storytime Under the Stars**
   If it's evening and the stars are shining, turn your fort into a cozy storytelling spot! Bring in your favorite books, or make up your own stories about adventures in the woods or space. Use your flashlight or fairy lights to create a magical ambiance while you read.

Story Idea: Imagine you're a brave explorer who discovers a hidden treasure deep in the forest. What kind of treasure do you find? Who else is there?

3. **Create a Nature Journal**
Grab a notebook and use your fort as a quiet space to draw or write about your outdoor adventures. You can sketch the plants and animals you see or write stories about the creatures that live in your backyard.
Bonus Idea: Decorate your journal with leaves, flowers, and small drawings to make it feel special!

4. **Outdoor Snack Time**
Make your fort the perfect spot for a snack break. Bring in some healthy snacks like fruit, trail mix, or sandwiches, and enjoy a picnic inside your fort. If you want to get really adventurous, try making **s'mores** using a safe, supervised method, like a campfire or a portable fire pit.
Snack Challenge: Create a themed snack that matches your fort. If you built a pirate fort, make "treasure" cookies or "ocean" punch with blue drinks!

5. **Pretend Play and Role-Playing**
Use your fort for imaginative play! You can act out being a pirate captain, a superhero on a mission, or even an animal in the wild. Create characters and adventures with your friends or siblings.
Character Ideas:
   - Pirate Captain Jack and his crew
   - Superhero with magical powers
   - Forest animals on a quest to find food

Weather Watch: Keep an Eye on the Sky!

Since you're building outdoor forts, it's super important to keep an eye on the weather. Here are some tips for watching the weather while you enjoy your fort:

1. **Sunny Days**
If it's a bright, sunny day, make sure to stay hydrated. Bring a water bottle into your fort, and take breaks in the shade when you need to cool off. You can use your fort to create a shady spot to relax and enjoy the breeze!

2. **Windy Days**
If it's a bit windy, make sure your fort is secure. Check that all the branches and sticks are tight, and use rocks to weigh down anything that might blow away. If it gets too windy, you might want to wait for a calmer day to enjoy your fort.

3. **Rainy Days**
If it looks like rain is coming, it's time to be smart! Make sure your fort has a good cover, like a tarp or blankets, to keep you dry. If the rain gets heavy, it's best to pack up your fort and head inside to avoid getting soaked. Always make sure to clean up any supplies so they don't get ruined by the rain!

4. **Cloud Watching**
   On a nice, cloudy day, lying inside your fort and looking up at the clouds can be super fun! Try to find shapes in the clouds and see if you can guess what they look like. You can even have a "cloud naming" contest with your friends!

Adventure Time: Exploring the Area Around Your Fort

While your fort is super fun, don't forget to explore the area around it! Here are some exciting outdoor adventures you can have nearby:

1. **Bug Safari**
   Go on a bug safari! Look around your fort and see how many different bugs you can find. Make a list of the bugs you see and try to identify them. You can also build a mini habitat for your favorite bug using leaves and sticks!
   Bug Bingo: Create a bingo card with different bugs you might find, and see if you can spot them all!
2. **Nature Walks**
   Explore the area around your fort. Take a nature walk to see what plants, flowers, or animals you can find. Bring a camera or your phone to take pictures of interesting things you see along the way!
3. **Nature Art**
   Collect leaves, twigs, flowers, and stones to create some nature art! Use your finds to make patterns, designs, or even sculptures. You can stick them to your fort walls or create an art display outside.
4. **Tree Climbing Adventures**
   If there are safe trees nearby, try climbing up into them to get a better view of the area. Just be sure to ask an adult for help, and don't climb too high!

The Great Outdoor Fort Contest

Once you've built your fort and tested it out, why not have a friendly contest? Invite your friends or family to see who can build the coolest outdoor fort! Here's how to organize the contest:

1. **Set a Time Limit**
   Decide how long everyone has to build their fort. Maybe 30 minutes or an hour is a good amount of time!
2. **Have Judges**
   If you have enough people, choose a couple of judges who will walk around and see each fort. They can check out the creativity, size, and any special features.
3. **Award Fun Prizes**
   Create fun awards for each fort. You could have categories like "Most Creative," "Tallest

Fort," or "Best Secret Features." Give out little prizes like stickers, treats, or homemade certificates to the winners!

Wrapping Up: Outdoor Adventures Await!

Building outdoor forts is all about **embracing nature**, having fun, and letting your imagination run wild. You've learned how to build different types of outdoor forts, weatherproof them, and make your fort a super fun hangout spot. Plus, with all the exciting activities and challenges, you'll never run out of things to do.

In the next chapter, we're going to explore **advanced fort construction**, where we'll learn how to add multi-room designs and hidden spaces to make your fort even more awesome! But for now, get out there, build your fort, and enjoy all the fun adventures waiting for you in nature!

Make a Difference with Your Review

Unlock the Power of Generosity

"True happiness is found in helping others." - Anonymous

Hello, wonderful readers! Thank you for joining me on this journey towards a more active and joyful life with "How to Build the Best Fort Ever." I'm Ashton Gunnell, and I poured my heart into creating this book to help every kid enjoy the joy of building awesome forts.

Now, I have a small favor to ask...

Would you help someone you've never met, even if you never got credit for it?

Who is this person? They are just like you. Or, at least, like you used to be. They're eager to follow the guide for building the BEST forts inside and outside.

Our mission is to make it possible for all kids to have the opportunity to build incredible forts. Everything I do stems from that mission. And the only way to reach everyone is with your help.

Most people do, in fact, judge a book by its cover (and its reviews). So here's my ask on behalf of a senior you've never met:

Please help that senior by leaving this book a review.

Your gift costs no money and takes less than 60 seconds to make real, but it can change a child's life forever. Your review could help...

- **Unleash Your Creativity**: Discover endless possibilities for fort building! This book provides fun ideas and step-by-step instructions to transform your space into incredible forts, inspiring your imagination and creativity.
- **Endless Fun Activities**: From themed forts to exciting games and sleepovers, this book is packed with activities that will keep you and your friends entertained for hours. Create unforgettable memories as you embark on countless adventures!
- **Safe and Engaging Learning**: Learn important safety tips and teamwork skills while having a blast! This book emphasizes safe fort building practices, ensuring a fun and enjoyable experience for everyone involved.

To get that 'feel good' feeling and help this person for real, all you have to do is leave a review, and it takes less than 60 seconds.

Scan the QR code below to leave your review:

[https://www.amazon.com/review/review-your-purchases/?asin=BOOKASIN]

If you feel good about helping another senior, you are my kind of person. Welcome to the club. You're one of us.

I'm even more excited to help you achievethe ability and fun of designing, build and constructing the best fort possible. You'll love the step by step process and tips I'll share in the coming pages.

Thank you from the bottom of my heart. Now, back to our regularly scheduled programming.

- Your biggest fan, Ashton Gunnell

PS - Fun fact: If you provide something of value to another person, it makes you more valuable to them. If you'd like goodwill straight from another senior - and you believe this book will help them - send it their way.

Chapter 5: Advanced Fort Construction: Multi-Room & Hidden Spaces

Hey there, Fort Architects!

Congratulations on all your amazing fort-building skills so far! Now that you've mastered the classic blanket fort and outdoor forts, it's time to take things up a notch and become a true **fort architect**. In this chapter, we'll learn how to build **multi-room forts** and add **hidden spaces** to your creations.

Just like a real castle or secret hideout, your fort can have multiple rooms, secret doors, and cool compartments that make it feel like a real adventure. Are you ready to make your fort the ultimate hideaway? Let's get started!

Expanding Your Fort: Multi-Room Designs

Building a fort with multiple rooms can make it feel more exciting and spacious. Just like a house or castle, each room can have its own purpose! Here's how to create a multi-room fort:

How to Create a Multi-Room Fort

1. **Plan Your Layout**
   Before you start building, it helps to have a plan. Think about how many rooms you want and what each one will be for. Here are some room ideas:

- ○ **The Main Room**: This is where everyone hangs out. It can have pillows, snacks, and maybe a movie setup.
- ○ **The Secret Room**: A cozy spot for quiet time or reading.
- ○ **The Snack Room**: A designated area just for food and drinks.
- ○ **The Lookout Room**: A higher spot where you can peek out and see what's going on outside!

2. **Set Up the Walls**

   Use blankets, pillows, and furniture to create walls for each room. You can use tall chairs or couches to separate the spaces. Drape blankets across the chairs to make walls that you can easily move through.

   Pro Tip: Leave a little space between the walls of the rooms to create doorways. This way, you can walk freely between rooms without needing to crawl out of the fort every time!

3. **Add the Roof**

   Once you've set up the walls, drape a big blanket over the whole structure to create a roof. Make sure it's supported well so it doesn't sag too much! You can also use more chairs or a table to help hold the blanket up.

4. **Create Openings Between Rooms**

   For a true multi-room experience, create openings where you can crawl from one room to another. You can leave gaps in the walls or make small "doorways" by rolling up a blanket. This makes it easy to move around your fort!

5. **Decorate Each Room**

   Now comes the fun part! Decorate each room according to its purpose. Use pillows, stuffed animals, lights, and any other fun decorations you can find. You can even give each room a name and put up a sign to tell everyone what it is!

   Example Room Names:
   - ○ "Pirate Treasure Room"
   - ○ "Superhero Hideout"
   - ○ "Cozy Reading Nook"

Secret Entrances & Hidden Passages

Now that you've built a multi-room fort, let's add some mystery with **secret entrances** and **hidden passages**! These features will make your fort feel like a real adventure.

How to Create Secret Entrances

1. **The Hidden Doorway**

   Find a spot in your fort that can be the entrance to a secret room. You can use a blanket to hide the doorway. When someone walks by, they won't even see it! Just make sure to leave enough space for you to crawl in and out.

   Fun Idea: You can make a secret knock or password to enter this special room. Only your closest friends should know it!

2. **Tunnel to a Treasure Room**
   Create a tunnel from one room to another by using blankets and chairs. Set it up like a **secret passage**. Make sure it's big enough to crawl through but still feels like a secret!
   Tunnel Adventure: Pretend the tunnel leads to a treasure room filled with jewels (or candy) that you have to defend from pirates!
3. **Camouflaged Entrances**
   Use leaves, pillows, or blankets to camouflage your entrances. If someone is looking for you, they won't find your secret hideout! Make it a game to see who can spot your hidden door.
4. **Trapdoors**
   For the ultimate secret feature, create a **trapdoor** in your fort! You can use a large piece of cardboard or a blanket. Make sure to support it so it doesn't fall. When you're ready, lift it up to reveal a hidden space below!

Connecting Indoor and Outdoor Forts

If you've built both an indoor fort and an outdoor fort, why not **connect them**? Imagine having a whole fort complex with multiple rooms inside and outside. Here's how to bridge the gap:

1. **Create an Outdoor Escape**
   If you have an outdoor fort, make sure it has a hidden entrance leading inside your indoor fort. You can use a blanket tunnel or rope bridge to connect the two.
2. **The Sliding Entrance**
   Build a slide or a ramp that leads from your outdoor fort into your indoor fort. You can use a piece of cardboard or a sturdy blanket to create a slide. This makes it super fun to zoom back and forth between your two fort worlds!
3. **Secret Pathways**
   Use paths made of sticks, rocks, or even a rope to connect your outdoor and indoor forts. You can create little signs along the way that say, "Treasure Ahead" or "Secret Passage—Keep Out!" to make the adventure even more exciting.

Building Hidden Spaces: Where Adventure Awaits

Let's add some hidden spaces inside your multi-room fort! Hidden spots can be perfect for secrets, games, or just chilling out. Here's how to create these fun little areas:

How to Build Hidden Spaces

1. **Secret Compartments**
   Use pillows and blankets to create compartments where you can hide things. For example, stack pillows high and create a little space behind them to hide toys, snacks, or

notes.

Treasure Hunt: Leave clues in the hidden compartments for your friends to find! Create a scavenger hunt where they have to search for secret items.

2. **Curtain Walls**

   Use sheets or blankets as **curtains** to create hidden spaces. Hang them up on the inside walls to make secret hideaways that can be closed off. You can sneak in and out without anyone knowing where you went!

3. **Bunk Beds**

   If your fort is big enough, make a **bunk bed** using pillows or cushions stacked on top of each other. You can climb up and pretend you're sleeping in a castle high above the ground!

   Bunk Bed Adventure: Pretend you're in a treehouse or a pirate ship, sleeping high above the waves!

4. **Treasure Chests**

   Find a box or container that can act as a treasure chest inside your fort. Fill it with fun goodies like candy, toys, or special items. You can decorate the outside to make it look like a real treasure chest.

Fun Activities in Your Multi-Room Fort

Once you've built your multi-room fort with secret spaces, it's time to fill it with fun activities! Here are some ideas to keep the adventure going:

1. **Fort Movie Night**

   Set up a movie night in your fort with blankets, pillows, and snacks. Use a portable device or a tablet to watch your favorite films. Make sure each room has a cozy spot to sit and watch!

2. **Board Games and Card Games**

   Bring in some board games or card games to play with your friends. Each room can have a different game set up, and you can move from room to room as you play!

3. **Imagination Station**

   Turn your fort into an imagination station. Each room can be a different place, like a jungle, space station, or underwater world. Act out different adventures in each room!

4. **Treasure Hunt**

   Create a treasure hunt around your fort! Hide clues in each room and lead your friends on a quest to find the ultimate treasure (like snacks or a cool prize).

Wrapping Up: Your Fort Awaits!

Wow, you've learned so much about advanced fort-building! You're now a pro at creating multi-room forts, adding secret entrances, and building hidden spaces. Your fort can be as imaginative and adventurous as you want it to be!

In the next chapter, we'll talk about **themed forts** and how to make your fort even more special with unique designs and decorations. But for now, gather your friends, start building, and let the fort adventures begin!

Chapter 6: Themed Forts: Adventure Awaits

Hey there, Fort Adventurers!

Are you ready to take your fort-building skills to the next level? In this chapter, we're diving into the world of **themed forts**! A themed fort is like stepping into a whole new world. You can transform your fort into a pirate ship, a magical castle, a jungle safari, or even a superhero hideout!

The best part about themed forts is that you get to use your imagination and creativity to make them super special. So grab your supplies, and let's explore some awesome themed fort ideas together!

---

1. Pirate Ship Fort: Ahoy, Matey!

Who doesn't want to sail the seas on a pirate ship? With a little creativity, your fort can become the ultimate pirate ship where you can go on treasure hunts and search for buried gold! Here's how to build your own **pirate ship fort**:

How to Build a Pirate Ship Fort

1. **Gather Your Supplies**
   You'll need blankets, pillows, chairs, cardboard, and anything that looks like it could be part of a pirate ship. You can also find pirate-themed decorations like flags or maps!
2. **Set Up the Ship Frame**
   Use chairs to create the base of your ship. Set them up in a circle or a square to form the ship's hull. Make sure there's enough space for you and your pirate crew to move around inside.
3. **Build the Sails**
   Drape a large blanket or sheet over the top of the chairs to make the sail of your ship. If you have cardboard, you can cut it into a triangle shape and attach it to the top of the fort to make it look like a sail.
   Pirate Tip: Draw a skull and crossbones on a piece of paper and tape it to the front of your fort to make it look like the Jolly Roger flag!
4. **Create a Treasure Chest**
   Use a box to create a treasure chest inside your pirate fort. Fill it with snacks, toys, or shiny objects (like coins) to represent your treasure.
5. **Set Sail for Adventure!**
   Once your pirate ship fort is ready, gather your crew (friends or family), grab some eye patches, and set off on a pirate adventure! You can pretend to hunt for treasure or battle rival pirates!

---

2. Jungle Safari Fort: Roar like a Lion!

Let's travel deep into the jungle and create an amazing **jungle safari fort**! With this fort, you can pretend to be an explorer searching for wild animals and hidden treasures. Here's how to make your own jungle fort:

How to Build a Jungle Safari Fort

1. **Collect Jungle Supplies**
   Gather green blankets, pillows, stuffed animals (like lions and monkeys), and any other jungle-themed decorations. You can also use real leaves or branches if you have them!
2. **Create the Jungle Base**
   Use chairs to make the structure of your fort. Place them in a circle or in a way that creates a cave-like entrance.
3. **Add Jungle Vines**
   Drape green blankets or sheets around your fort to create the feeling of vines hanging in the jungle. You can even tie pieces of yarn or rope to look like vines!
4. **Make Animal Sounds**
   Bring in your stuffed animals and place them around the fort. You can add sounds by playing animal noises on a phone or tablet, or just have fun pretending to roar like a lion!

5. **Go on a Safari Adventure!**
   Once your jungle fort is ready, invite your friends for a safari adventure! Pretend to discover wild animals, search for treasure, or go on an expedition through the jungle!

3. Princess Castle Fort: A Royal Adventure!

Every kid dreams of living in a castle! With a **princess castle fort**, you can pretend to be royalty, host royal tea parties, or protect your kingdom from dragons! Here's how to create your magical castle fort:

How to Build a Princess Castle Fort

1. **Gather Castle Supplies**
   You'll need blankets, cushions, pillows, cardboard, and anything sparkly or royal-looking! You can also grab a tiara or dress-up clothes for a special touch.
2. **Build the Castle Walls**
   Use chairs to form the walls of your castle. You can arrange them in a square or circle to create the main room of your castle.
3. **Create the Towers**
   To make towers, stack pillows or cushions on top of each other in the corners of your fort. You can drape blankets over the tops to make them look like castle turrets!
4. **Decorate the Castle**
   Use your sparkly decorations to add royal flair to your fort. You can hang drawings or paper crowns on the walls to make it feel magical.
5. **Host a Royal Tea Party**
   Once your castle is complete, invite your friends for a royal tea party! Bring in snacks, drinks, and pretend you're having a fancy gathering with knights and princesses!

---

4. Superhero Hideout: Save the Day!

Do you have a favorite superhero? Now you can create a **superhero hideout** where you and your friends can plan missions and save the world! Here's how to build your own superhero fort:

How to Build a Superhero Hideout

1. **Gather Your Superhero Gear**
   You'll need blankets, pillows, and any superhero toys or decorations. You can also make superhero capes using old t-shirts or fabric!
2. **Set Up Your Hideout**
   Use chairs and blankets to create a big, open space. You can set the chairs in a circle or line them up to form a "base."
3. **Create a Control Center**
   Use cardboard boxes to make control panels. You can draw buttons and screens on the boxes with markers. This will be your superhero control center!
4. **Design Your Superhero Logos**
   Grab some paper and draw your superhero logos. Tape them up around your fort to make it feel like a real hideout.
5. **Plan Your Missions!**
   Once your superhero hideout is ready, gather your friends and plan some superhero missions. You can pretend to save the day, fight villains, or protect your city from danger!

---

5. Space Station Fort: Blast Off into Adventure!

It's time to journey to the stars with a **space station fort**! In this fort, you can pretend to be astronauts exploring the galaxy. Here's how to create your own space station:

How to Build a Space Station Fort

1. **Gather Space Supplies**
   You'll need silver or dark blankets, pillows, and anything that looks space-themed, like glow-in-the-dark stars or planets!
2. **Build the Space Station Base**
   Use chairs to create the main area of your space station. Arrange them to make a big round space where everyone can sit.
3. **Create the Control Room**
   Drape a dark blanket over the top of the chairs to create a roof. Use cardboard boxes to make "control panels" and draw buttons on them.
4. **Decorate with Stars and Planets**
   Hang glow-in-the-dark stars from the ceiling or walls. You can also cut out paper planets and tape them to the walls to make it feel like you're in outer space.
5. **Launch into Adventure!**
   Once your space station is ready, invite your friends for an outer space adventure! You can pretend to explore new planets, meet alien creatures, or blast off into the galaxy!

Final Thoughts: Your Themed Fort Adventure Awaits!

Now you're ready to build some of the most awesome themed forts ever! Whether you're sailing the seas as a pirate, exploring the jungle, hosting a royal tea party, saving the world as a superhero, or blasting off into space, each themed fort opens up a world of adventure and fun.

Remember, the best part of fort building is using your imagination and making it your own. So grab your friends, choose your theme, and let the adventure begin!

In the next chapter, we'll talk about **fort safety** to make sure you have a safe and fun time while you play. But for now, get out there and start building your amazing themed fort!

Chapter 7: Fort Safety: Keeping Fun Safe

Hey there, Fort Builders!

Welcome to the **Safety Zone**! As you embark on your awesome fort-building adventures, it's super important to remember that safety comes first. Forts are places of imagination and fun, but we want to make sure everyone stays safe while playing.

In this chapter, we'll cover some essential tips for keeping your forts safe, whether you're building inside your house or outside in nature. So grab your hard hats (just kidding, but it helps to be smart), and let's get ready to learn how to keep the fun going without any bumps or bruises!

---

1. Indoor Safety: Making Your Fort a Safe Haven

When you're building forts indoors, there are a few things to keep in mind to avoid accidents and make your fort a cozy and safe space.

How to Stay Safe While Fort Building Indoors

1. **Choose a Safe Location**
   Pick a spot in your house that's away from sharp corners, furniture, or anything that can fall over. Living rooms, playrooms, or bedrooms are great places to build forts because they usually have soft floors and plenty of space.
2. **Watch Out for Tripping Hazards**
   When setting up your fort, make sure there aren't any toys, shoes, or other items on the floor that could trip you or your friends while you're crawling in and out. Keep the area around your fort clear!
   Tip: You can make a fun game out of it by pretending you're a treasure hunter and the floor is a jungle full of traps!
3. **Secure Your Structure**
   Make sure all blankets and pillows are secured so they don't fall while you're inside. You can use clips or rubber bands to keep everything in place. If you notice something feels wobbly, adjust it before you climb in!
4. **Avoid Heavy Objects**
   Be careful not to place heavy objects on top of your fort. If you're using things like boxes, make sure they're lightweight so they won't hurt anyone if they fall.
5. **Set a Fort Time Limit**
   If you're planning to hang out in your fort for a while, set a time limit so you don't get too restless or cramped. You can take breaks to stretch, grab snacks, or do some fun activities outside your fort!

---

2. Outdoor Safety: Exploring Nature Responsibly

Building forts outdoors is an incredible adventure, but there are some important safety rules to follow to make sure your playtime in nature is fun and safe!

How to Stay Safe While Fort Building Outdoors

1. **Choose the Right Spot**
   When picking a place to build your outdoor fort, look for a flat area that's clear of rocks, thorny bushes, and sharp objects. Avoid building under trees with low-hanging branches or near water.
   Pro Tip: Find a spot with some shade to keep you cool while you play!
2. **Check for Bugs and Critters**
   Before you start building, check the area for any bugs, ants, or critters. Make sure there's nothing that could bite or sting you while you're building. If you find a beehive or ant hill, it's best to build your fort somewhere else!
3. **Keep an Eye on the Weather**
   Always check the weather before you go outside. If it's too hot, too windy, or raining, it might be better to stay indoors. If you see dark clouds, be sure to pack up your fort and head inside before it rains.
4. **Stay Hydrated**
   When you're outside playing, it's super important to drink water. Bring a water bottle to your fort so you can stay hydrated while you're having fun. You don't want to get too hot or tired!
5. **Play with Friends**
   It's always safer to build forts with friends or family. Not only is it more fun, but it also means someone is there to help if you need it. Plus, you can work together to create a really awesome fort!

---

3. Weather Considerations: When to Build and When to Stay Inside

The weather can change quickly, so it's important to know when it's a good time to build your fort and when it's best to stay inside.

Building Forts in Different Weather Conditions

1. **Sunny Days**
   Sunny days are perfect for building outdoor forts! Just remember to wear sunscreen and take breaks in the shade to avoid getting too hot. Don't forget to drink plenty of water!
2. **Windy Days**
   If it's super windy, be careful when building outdoor forts. Strong winds can blow your fort down! If it's just a light breeze, make sure to weigh down your fort with rocks, but if it's really windy, it might be better to stay inside.

3. **Rainy Days**
   If you see rain in the forecast, it's best to avoid building outdoor forts. Rain can make everything wet and slippery, which isn't safe. Instead, focus on creating the ultimate indoor fort!
4. **Stormy Weather**
   If there are thunderstorms or severe weather warnings, stay inside and avoid building outdoor forts altogether. Safety is the most important thing, and you can always build forts another day!

---

4. Playing Safely Inside Your Fort

Once you've built your fort, it's time to have fun! But it's still important to remember some safety tips while you play inside your fort.

How to Play Safely Inside Your Fort

1. **Set Up a "No Running" Rule**
   Inside your fort, it's best to keep it a no-running zone! Crawling and walking are great ways to move around without bumping into things or knocking over your fort.
2. **Avoid Heavy Lifting**
   When you're inside your fort, avoid lifting heavy objects or moving chairs around. If you need to change something, ask a friend for help to avoid any accidents.
3. **Create a Quiet Time**
   If your fort is getting crowded, set aside some quiet time where everyone can relax and enjoy some peaceful moments. This is a great time for reading, drawing, or telling stories without getting too loud.
4. **Keep Snacks and Drinks Away from Electronics**
   If you're using any electronic devices inside your fort, like a tablet or phone, keep snacks and drinks far away to prevent spills. You can create a designated snack zone outside your fort instead!
5. ****Use Flash lights Wisely****
   If you're using flashlights or other light sources inside your fort, make sure to point them away from anyone's face. It's best to keep lights low so you can see without blinding each other.

---

5. Emergency Plans: Be Prepared for Anything!

It's always a good idea to have an emergency plan in case something goes wrong while you're playing in or around your fort. Here are some simple steps to ensure everyone stays safe:

How to Prepare for Emergencies

1. **Set a Meeting Spot**
   Before you start playing, choose a safe spot nearby where everyone can meet if you need to leave the fort quickly. This could be a tree, a nearby bench, or the door to your house.
2. **Know Your Phone's Location**
   If you have a phone with you, make sure you know where it is. You can ask an adult to keep it nearby in case you need to call for help.
3. **Identify the Nearest Adult**
   Make sure you know where an adult is while you're playing outside. If you need help or feel unsafe, you can easily go to them for support.
4. **Practice Communication**
   Have a code word or signal with your friends that means it's time to stop playing or that someone needs help. This way, you can alert each other quickly without causing panic.
5. **Discuss "What If" Scenarios**
   Talk with your friends about different situations and how you would handle them. For example, "What would we do if it starts raining?" or "What if someone feels sick?" This helps everyone feel prepared and safe.

---

6. Cleaning Up: Keep Your Space Safe and Neat

After you've had a blast building and playing in your fort, it's important to clean up! Keeping your play area neat is part of being a responsible fort builder. Here's how to make cleanup a breeze:

How to Clean Up Safely

1. **Make It a Team Effort**
   If you built your fort with friends, make cleanup a team activity! Everyone can help pick up blankets, pillows, and other supplies, making it quicker and more fun.
2. **Return Borrowed Items**
   If you used items that belong to others (like blankets from the couch), return them to their rightful places. This helps keep your space neat and your parents happy!
3. **Check for Trash**
   After snacking or playing, be sure to pick up any wrappers, crumbs, or leftover snacks. A clean fort area is a happy fort area!
4. **Store Supplies Properly**
   Once everything is clean, put your supplies away in their designated spots. This helps you stay organized for the next time you want to build a fort!
5. **Inspect Your Fort Area**
   Before you leave, take a look around to ensure everything is safe and tidy. Make sure there are no tripping hazards or leftover materials that could cause someone to stumble.

7. Involve Your Friends and Family

Finally, remember that fort building is even more fun when you include your friends and family. Talk to them about fort safety, so everyone knows what to expect and how to keep each other safe while having a blast!

How to Make Fort Building a Group Activity

1. **Share Safety Tips**
   Before you start building, share the safety tips you've learned with your friends and family. Everyone will feel more comfortable and know how to play safely.
2. **Create a Fort Code of Conduct**
   Work together to create a fun "Fort Code of Conduct" that includes safety rules everyone agrees to follow. This can be a silly list of rules, like "No running in the fort" or "Always help each other clean up!"
3. **Encourage Teamwork**
   Building forts can be a great team-building exercise. Encourage everyone to work together, whether they're helping to build, decorate, or come up with creative ideas for the fort.
4. **Invite Your Family to Play**
   Don't forget to invite your family members to check out your fort! They might have their own stories or experiences to share, and you can all have fun together inside your amazing creation.

Wrapping Up: Safety is Key!

Now you're armed with all the safety knowledge you need to have the best fort-building adventures ever! Remember, safety is super important whether you're indoors or outdoors. By following these tips, you'll keep the fun going without any worries.

In the next chapter, we're going to explore all the exciting games and activities you can play inside your fort. But for now, stay safe, have fun, and let your imagination run wild in your awesome forts!

Chapter 8: Games and Activities Inside Your Fort

Hey there, Fort Adventurers!

Congratulations on building the most amazing forts ever! Now that you've created your cozy spaces, it's time to fill them with **fun activities and games**. Whether you're inside an indoor fort or lounging in your outdoor hideaway, there are endless possibilities for adventure and imagination.

In this chapter, we'll explore tons of exciting games, creative activities, and fun ideas to make the most of your fort experience. Get ready for some action-packed fun that will keep you and your friends entertained for hours!

---

1. Imagination Games: Create Your Own Adventures

Imagination is the best part of fort play! With a little creativity, you can turn your fort into a world of adventures. Here are some fun imagination games to play with friends:

A. The Royal Quest

What You Need:

- Your fort set up as a castle
- Costumes or props (crowns, capes, etc.)
- A list of quests

How to Play:

1. **Set the Scene:**
   Decorate your fort to look like a royal castle. Use blankets, cushions, and any sparkly items you can find to create a majestic atmosphere.
2. **Choose Your Roles:**
   Decide who will be the king or queen and who will be the knights or princesses. You can even include dragons or magical creatures if you want!
3. **Create Quests:**
   Write down a list of quests that need to be completed. These could include finding hidden treasures, rescuing a stuffed animal from a dragon, or solving a riddle.
4. **Embark on Your Quest:**
   Use your imaginations to complete each quest. You can create obstacles or challenges along the way. For example, you might have to "cross a dangerous bridge" (a blanket stretched across two chairs) or "fight off dragons" (stuffed animals that you pretend to battle).
5. **Celebrate Your Victory:**
   Once you've completed all the quests, gather in your fort to celebrate your victory with a royal feast of snacks!

B. Superhero Showdown

What You Need:

- Superhero costumes or props

- A designated area in your fort

How to Play:

1. **Create Your Characters:**
   Each person chooses a superhero character. You can be your favorite superhero or even invent your own! Give your character a name and special powers.
2. **Set the Scene:**
   Turn your fort into a superhero headquarters. Use pillows to create "training areas" and "labs" where you can plan your superhero missions.
3. **Plan Missions:**
   Write down different superhero missions that you can go on. These could include saving a toy from danger, stopping a villain (one of your friends pretending to be a bad guy), or retrieving stolen treasures.
4. **Act Out Your Missions:**
   Use your imagination to act out each mission. Create dramatic moments, heroic saves, and epic battles as you play.
5. **Share Your Stories:**
   After completing your missions, gather in your fort to share stories of your heroic adventures and celebrate your bravery!

2. Movie Night in Your Fort: Cozy Film Experience

What's better than watching a movie in your super cozy fort? Movie nights are perfect for spending time with friends and family while enjoying your favorite films.

How to Set Up Movie Night

What You Need:

- A portable device (tablet, phone, or laptop)

- Blankets and pillows for seating
- Snacks (popcorn, candy, etc.)
- Fairy lights or flashlights for ambiance

Steps to Create the Ultimate Movie Night:

1. **Create Your Movie Space:**
   Make your fort extra cozy with plenty of pillows and blankets. Set up your screen (tablet or laptop) at a comfortable viewing height.
2. **Decorate with Lights:**
   Use string lights or flashlights to create a magical atmosphere inside your fort. Dim the lights (if possible) to make it feel like a real movie theater!
3. **Prepare Your Snacks:**
   Gather your favorite movie snacks! Popcorn, chips, candy, and drinks are all great choices. Set up a little snack station outside your fort or bring them inside for easy access.
4. **Pick Your Movies:**
   Choose a few of your favorite movies to watch. You can have a themed movie marathon—like superhero movies, animated films, or adventure flicks.
5. **Enjoy the Show:**
   Once everything is set up, sit back, relax, and enjoy your movie! You can even pause the movie to discuss funny moments or act out scenes.

---

3. Fort Challenges: Timed Building Contests

Ready for a fun competition? Fort challenges are a great way to see who can build the coolest fort in a limited amount of time.

How to Organize a Fort Challenge

What You Need:

- A timer
- Building supplies (blankets, chairs, pillows)
- A group of friends or family

Steps to Host the Ultimate Fort Challenge:

1. **Set the Rules:**
   Decide on the rules for the challenge. For example, how long will each person have to build their fort? Will there be a theme for the forts?
2. **Gather Supplies:**
   Collect all the supplies you'll need for building. Make sure everyone has access to blankets, pillows, and any other materials.

3. **Start the Timer:**
   Once everyone is ready, set the timer for the agreed-upon time (like 20 or 30 minutes).
4. **Build Your Forts:**
   Let everyone start building their forts! Encourage creativity and teamwork, and remind everyone to keep it fun.
5. **Judging Time:**
   Once the time is up, have everyone show off their forts! You can either judge them based on creativity, size, and design, or invite friends or family to vote for their favorite.
6. **Celebrate Everyone's Efforts:**
   After the challenge, gather together and celebrate everyone's hard work with snacks and storytelling inside the forts!

---

4. Storytime Adventures: Sharing Tales in Your Fort

Inside your fort is the perfect place for storytelling! Whether you're reading books, sharing personal stories, or creating new tales, storytime can spark your imagination and bring everyone together.

How to Host a Storytime Adventure

What You Need:

- Books or notebooks
- Flashlights or fairy lights
- Cozy seating in your fort

Steps to Create a Magical Storytime:

1. **Set Up a Cozy Space:**
   Arrange pillows and blankets in your fort to make a comfy seating area. Make sure there's enough room for everyone to sit and enjoy the stories.
2. **Create a Warm Atmosphere:**
   Dim the lights inside your fort with fairy lights or use flashlights to create a warm and inviting glow.
3. **Choose Your Stories:**
   You can either read from a book or take turns sharing personal stories. If you want to get creative, try telling an improvised story where each person adds a sentence to build a tale together.
4. **Encourage Imagination:**
   If you're making up stories, encourage everyone to be silly and imaginative. You can create characters, settings, and plot twists on the spot!

5. **Act It Out:**
   For a fun twist, act out parts of the stories! Use props from around your fort or pretend you're in the story as you narrate.

---

5. Craft Corner: Create Art in Your Fort

Get creative in your fort with arts and crafts! This is a fantastic way to express your imagination and make something special.

How to Set Up a Craft Corner in Your Fort

What You Need:

- Art supplies (paper, markers, crayons, stickers, glue)
- Craft materials (scissors, magazines, fabric scraps)
- A flat surface (small table or clipboard)

Steps to Create Your Craft Corner:

1. **Gather Your Supplies:**
   Collect all the art and craft supplies you'll need. Make sure to have enough materials for everyone if you're crafting with friends.
2. **Set Up a Craft Table:**
   Use a small table, clipboard, or a flat surface to create your craft station inside the fort. This will be where everyone works on their projects.
3. **Choose Your Craft Projects:**
   Decide what you want to make! You could create friendship bracelets, drawings, collages, or even decorate picture frames.
4. **Get Crafting:**
   Let the creativity flow! Work on your projects while chatting and enjoying the cozy atmosphere of your fort.
5. **Show Off Your Art:**
   Once everyone is done, share your creations with the group! You can hang your artwork on the fort walls using tape or string to display your masterpieces.

6. Fort Olympics: Fun and Games Inside Your Fort

Why not create your own **Fort Olympics**? This is a great way to add some friendly competition to your fort experience while staying active and having fun.

How to Organize Your Fort Olympics

What You Need:

- Space inside your fort or nearby

- Various supplies for games (balls, pillows, etc.)
- A timer or stopwatch

Steps to Host Your Fort Olympics:

1. **Choose Your Events:**
   Decide what games and challenges you want to include in your Fort Olympics. Here are some fun ideas:
   - **Pillow Toss:** See who can toss a pillow into a designated area.
   - **Obstacle Course:** Set up a mini obstacle course using pillows, chairs, and blankets. Time each participant to see who can complete it the fastest!
- **Fort Relay Race:** Have teams race to build a small section of a fort using only one hand. Switch after a set time to complete your sections.
- **Silly Walks Race:** Have a race where everyone must walk in silly ways (like hopping, crawling, or tiptoeing) to the finish line.
2. **Set Up Your Area:**
   Make sure you have enough space inside your fort or in a safe area nearby to play your games. Clear away any obstacles to ensure everyone can participate without tripping.
3. **Create Your Rules:**
   Before starting, establish clear rules for each game. Make sure everyone understands how to play and what the objectives are. Keep the rules simple and fun!
4. **Time the Events:**
   Use a stopwatch or timer to time each event. If you're doing a relay race, make sure everyone knows when to go!
5. **Keep Score:**
   Decide how you'll keep score for each event. You can assign points for first, second, and third places or just have fun without keeping score at all!
6. **Celebrate the Winners:**
   Once all the events are complete, gather everyone to celebrate! You can give out fun awards or certificates for participation or special achievements like "Best Sportsmanship" or "Silliest Walker."

---

7. Fort Camping: A Sleepover Adventure

If you want to take your fort experience to the next level, why not turn it into a camping adventure? You can set up a fort for an overnight stay, complete with sleeping bags and snacks.

How to Host a Fort Camping Adventure

What You Need:

- Sleeping bags or blankets
- Snacks (like marshmallows, popcorn, or s'mores)

- Flashlights or lanterns
- A cozy space in your fort

Steps for Your Fort Camping Adventure:

1. **Set Up Your Sleeping Area:**
   Inside your fort, spread out sleeping bags or blankets to create a comfy sleeping area. Make sure everyone has enough room to lie down.
2. **Prepare Camp Snacks:**
   Pack some fun snacks for your camping adventure! You can bring in marshmallows (and if you're allowed, make them over a safe, supervised campfire), popcorn, or make s'mores using the microwave or a campfire.
3. **Create a Campfire Atmosphere:**
   If you can, set up a small, safe "campfire" area outside your fort using candles or a battery-operated lantern. This will create a cozy atmosphere while you enjoy your snacks.
4. **Tell Campfire Stories:**
   As night falls, gather around your campfire area or inside your fort and share stories. These could be spooky tales, funny adventures, or even stories about your dreams and imaginations.
5. **Stargazing (if outside):**
   If you're outside, take a moment to look at the stars. Lie back on your sleeping bags and see if you can spot constellations. You can even use a stargazing app on a phone to help identify stars and planets!
6. **Have a Sleepover:**
   If you're camping overnight, enjoy your sleepover adventure! Share secrets, whisper about your favorite superheroes, or plan your next fort-building adventure as you drift off to sleep.

---

8. DIY Science Experiments Inside Your Fort

Why not turn your fort into a science lab for a day? You can conduct fun experiments while being cozy inside your fort.

How to Host Science Experiments in Your Fort

What You Need:

- Simple science experiment supplies (baking soda, vinegar, food coloring, etc.)
- Clear plastic containers or cups
- Craft supplies (if you're doing DIY science)

Steps for Your Science Adventure:

1. **Choose Your Experiments:**
   Look up some easy science experiments you can do with common household items. Here are a few fun ideas:
   - **Volcano Eruption:** Use baking soda and vinegar to create a fizzing volcano.
   - **Colorful Milk Swirls:** Use milk, food coloring, and dish soap to create swirling colors.
   - **DIY Lava Lamp:** Fill a bottle with water and add vegetable oil, then drop in food coloring for a colorful show!
2. **Set Up Your Science Lab:**
   Make a designated area in your fort for your experiments. Cover the area with newspaper or a towel to catch any spills.
3. **Gather Your Supplies:**
   Make sure you have everything you need for your experiments. Read the instructions carefully and prepare your materials ahead of time.
4. **Conduct Your Experiments:**
   Follow the steps for each experiment, and make sure to have fun! Discuss what you see and observe during each experiment with your friends.
5. **Share Your Results:**
   After completing your experiments, gather everyone in your fort and share what you discovered. You can even keep a "science journal" to write down your findings!

---

9. Creative Writing and Drawing in Your Fort

Your fort can also be a fantastic space for creativity! Use this time to write stories or draw in a fun, relaxed environment.

How to Set Up a Creative Corner in Your Fort

What You Need:

- Paper and pens or pencils
- Drawing supplies (crayons, markers, colored pencils)
- A comfy space to sit

Steps for Your Creative Adventure:

1. **Create Your Writing/Drawing Area:**
   Set up a cozy spot with pillows and blankets where you can comfortably sit and work on your stories or drawings.

2. **Choose Your Creative Project:**
   Decide whether you want to write a story, create a comic book, or draw pictures. You can work individually or collaborate with friends.
3. **Inspire Each Other:**
   Share ideas and prompts to get your creative juices flowing. You can start with a fun sentence like, "Once upon a time, in a magical fort…" and let your imagination take over!
4. **Create Your Characters:**
   If you're writing a story, spend some time designing your characters. What do they look like? What are their names? What adventures will they go on?
5. **Showcase Your Work:**
   Once you've finished your writing or drawings, hang them up in your fort to create an art gallery! You can also read your stories aloud to your friends for feedback and fun.

---

10. Fort Music Party: Sing and Dance in Your Fort!

What's a fort without some awesome music? Hosting a music party inside your fort is a great way to celebrate your fort-building adventures.

How to Throw a Fort Music Party

What You Need:

- A portable speaker or device to play music
- Musical instruments (if you have them)
- Space to dance and sing

Steps for Your Musical Adventure:

1. **Set Up Your Music Space:**
   Clear a little area in your fort where everyone can stand up and dance. Make sure there's enough room for everyone to move around safely.
2. **Create a Playlist:**
   Pick your favorite songs or create a fun playlist that everyone can enjoy. You can include popular songs, dance tracks, or even silly songs to keep things lively.
3. **Plan Your Dance Moves:**
   Invite your friends to create fun dance moves to go along with the music. You can even have a mini dance-off to see who has the best moves!
4. **Play Musical Instruments:**
   If you have any musical instruments, bring them into the fort and have a jam session! You can create a band and play together.
5. **Karaoke Time:**
   Set up a karaoke session where everyone can take turns singing their favorite songs. Use your fort as the stage and encourage everyone to cheer for each other!

6. **Celebrate with a Dance Party:**
   Once you've had your fun with music, throw a mini dance party in your fort! Jump around, dance together, and enjoy the lively atmosphere!

Wrapping Up: The Fun Never Ends!

Now that you have a ton of exciting games and activities to fill your fort, the fun never has to end! Whether you're going on imaginative adventures, enjoying movie nights, conducting science experiments, or hosting a music party, your fort is the perfect place for laughter and creativity.

In the next chapter, we'll dive into **fort sleepovers** and how to make your fort experience even more memorable. But for now, gather your friends, choose your favorite activities, and let the fort fun begin!

Chapter 9: Fort Sleepovers and Picnics: Making It an Event

Hey, Fort Friends!

Are you ready for the ultimate fort adventure? In this chapter, we're going to talk about how to turn your amazing fort into a cozy sleepover spot and a fun picnic area! Sleepovers and picnics inside your fort are super exciting ways to make your fort experience even more special. So grab your favorite snacks, pillows, and friends, and let's get started!

---

1. Overnight Fort Adventures: Camping Inside Your Fort

There's nothing quite like having a sleepover in your fort! You can stay up late, share stories, play games, and create memories that will last a lifetime. Here's how to plan the perfect **overnight fort adventure**:

How to Prepare for Your Fort Sleepover

What You Need:

- Sleeping bags or blankets
- Pillows (the more, the better!)
- Snacks (like popcorn, cookies, or candy)
- Flashlights or lanterns
- Fun games or activities to keep you entertained

Steps for a Cozy Sleepover:

1. **Set Up Your Sleeping Area:**
   Make sure you have enough space for everyone to sleep comfortably. Lay out sleeping bags or blankets in your fort so everyone has a cozy spot to snuggle up.
2. **Gather Your Supplies:**
   Collect snacks, drinks, and any fun items you want to bring into your fort. You can even set up a "snack station" just outside your fort so everyone can grab goodies throughout the night.
3. **Create a Cozy Atmosphere:**
   Use fairy lights, lanterns, or flashlights to make your fort feel magical at night. Dim the lights and let the cozy glow fill your fort for an enchanting sleepover experience!
4. **Plan Your Activities:**
   Think of fun games and activities to do during your sleepover. You could play card games, tell stories, watch movies, or even do some silly challenges!
5. **Set Up a Nighttime Campfire (Optional):**
   If you're outside, consider having a mini campfire (supervised by an adult). Roast

marshmallows for s'mores or enjoy snacks around the campfire. If you're indoors, you can use a small candle or flashlight to mimic a campfire while sharing stories.

6. **Prepare for Bedtime:**

After all the fun, it's time to wind down. Choose a bedtime story to read together or have a little quiet time to relax. Make sure everyone is cozy and comfortable before saying goodnight!

2. Fort Picnics: Fun and Food Inside Your Fort

Who says you can't have a picnic inside your fort? Fort picnics are a fun way to enjoy delicious food in a cozy setting. Plus, you can make it a special event by inviting friends and family!

How to Host a Fort Picnic

What You Need:

- A picnic blanket or large towel
- Tasty picnic foods (sandwiches, fruits, snacks)
- Drinks (like juice boxes or water bottles)
- Fun games or activities to enjoy after eating

Steps to Set Up Your Fort Picnic:

1. **Prepare Your Picnic Area:**
   Spread out a picnic blanket or large towel inside your fort to create a comfy dining area. Make sure there's enough room for everyone to sit and eat together.
2. **Gather Your Food:**
   Prepare fun picnic foods like sandwiches, fruits, cheese, crackers, or even wraps! You can also include snacks like chips or cookies. Don't forget drinks—juice boxes are always a hit!
3. **Pack Your Picnic Basket:**
   Put all your picnic goodies in a basket or bag to make it feel special. You can even decorate the basket with colorful napkins or stickers!
4. **Set Up the Atmosphere:**
   Make your picnic feel special by adding some decorations. You could use flower petals, fun napkins, or even a little centerpiece like a small toy or stuffed animal.
5. **Enjoy Your Picnic:**
   Once everything is set up, gather with your friends or family to enjoy your delicious picnic feast. Share stories, play games, and enjoy the cozy atmosphere of your fort.
6. **Play Fun Picnic Games:**
   After eating, have fun playing games! Here are a few ideas:
   - **Picnic Bingo:** Create bingo cards with items you see around you or foods you're eating. Cross them off as you spot them!
   - **Outdoor Scavenger Hunt:** If you're outside, go on a scavenger hunt to find specific items in nature (like leaves, flowers, or bugs).
   - **Memory Sharing:** Share funny or interesting memories while you relax. It's a great way to bond and laugh together!

3. Overnight Challenges: Fort Olympics

If you're feeling adventurous, why not host your own **Fort Olympics** during your sleepover? It's a great way to keep everyone entertained and add a little friendly competition!

How to Host Fort Olympics During Sleepovers

What You Need:

- Various games and challenges
- Timer or stopwatch
- Paper and pencil for scoring
- Prizes for winners (stickers, homemade certificates, etc.)

Steps for Hosting Fort Olympics:

1. **Choose Your Events:**
   Decide on fun challenges that everyone can participate in. Here are some ideas:
   - **Pillow Toss:** See who can throw a pillow into a designated spot.
   - **Fort Relay Race:** Have a relay where teams race to build a section of the fort.
   - **Obstacle Course:** Set up a mini obstacle course using cushions, chairs, and other supplies.
2. **Set Up Your Scoring:**
   Create a simple scoring system. You can assign points for each event (1st place gets 5 points, 2nd gets 3, and 3rd gets 1) or just keep track of who wins each event.
3. **Time the Events:**
   Use a timer for each challenge to keep things exciting. Set a time limit for each game, and be ready to cheer for everyone!
4. **Celebrate the Winners:**
   After all the events, announce the winners and give out fun prizes. You can make homemade certificates that say things like "Ultimate Pillow Toss Champion" or "Obstacle Course Master."
5. **Enjoy a Fort Dance Party:**
   After the competition, celebrate with a dance party! Turn on some music and dance together inside your fort. It's a great way to wind down after a fun-filled night!

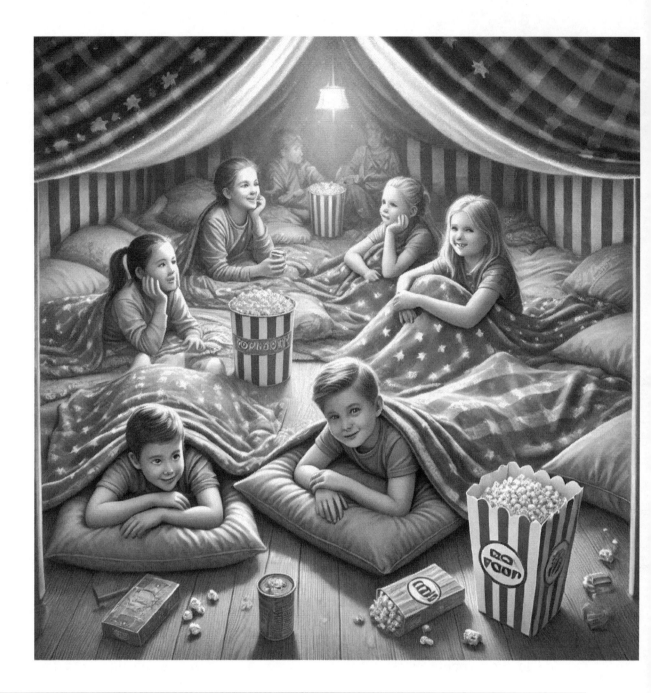

4. Fun Fort Sleepover Themes

To make your sleepover even more special, consider choosing a theme! Themes can help set the mood and make everything feel even more exciting. Here are some fun ideas for sleepover themes:

How to Create Fun Sleepover Themes

1. **Movie Marathon Night:**
   Choose a movie theme, like superhero movies or animated films. Everyone can dress up as their favorite character and watch movies that fit the theme.
2. **Camping Under the Stars:**
   Turn your fort into a camping site! Decorate with glow-in-the-dark stars, use sleeping bags, and tell spooky stories around a (fake) campfire.
3. **Pirate Adventure:**
   Go on a pirate adventure! Everyone can wear pirate costumes, and you can create a treasure map leading to hidden snacks around the house.
4. **Superhero Night:**
   Dress up as superheroes and share stories of your heroic adventures. You can even create your own superhero names and powers!
5. **Spa Night:**
   Have a relaxing spa-themed sleepover! Set up a "spa" area in your fort with face masks, nail polish, and calming music. Everyone can pamper themselves and relax together.

5. Creating Lasting Memories in Your Fort

While you're having fun with sleepovers and picnics, remember that these moments are special. Here are some ideas for capturing those memories and making your fort adventures unforgettable:

How to Create Lasting Memories:

1. **Memory Book:**
   Create a memory book during your sleepover. Use paper and pens to write down funny moments, stories, or drawings that represent your adventures. Everyone can contribute!
2. **Photo Scavenger Hunt:**
   Take pictures throughout your sleepover! Create a list of things to find and capture with your camera or phone. For example, find a silly face, a sleeping buddy, or a snack moment.
3. **Fort Journal:**
   Keep a fort journal where you write about your adventures, who you played with, and what you did. This can be a fun keepsake to look back on later.
4. **Decorate Your Fort:**
   After your sleepover, decorate your fort with drawings or fun signs that commemorate your time together. You can hang these up for future sleepovers!
5. **Thank You Notes:**
   After your adventure, write thank-you notes to your friends or family for joining you. It's a sweet way to show your appreciation and let them know how much fun you had!

Wrapping Up: The Adventure Continues!

Now you're all set to turn your fort into the ultimate sleepover and picnic destination! Whether you're having an overnight adventure, a cozy picnic, or Fort Olympics, the fun never ends when you're inside your fort.

In the next chapter, we'll explore how to take down and rebuild your fort, because the best part about fort building is that there's always a new adventure waiting. But for now, gather your friends, set up your fort sleepover or picnic, and make some amazing memories!

Chapter 10: Taking Down and Rebuilding: The Fun Continues

Hey, Fort Builders!

Congratulations on making it to the final chapter of your fort adventure! You've learned how to build the most amazing forts, fill them with fun activities, and enjoy sleepovers and picnics inside. Now it's time to talk about something just as exciting: **taking down your fort** and preparing for your next big build!

You might think that taking down a fort means the fun is over, but guess what? It's actually the start of a brand-new adventure! Let's explore how to safely dismantle your fort and why rebuilding can be just as much fun as building!

---

1. How to Safely Dismantle Your Fort

After all the fun and games, you'll want to take down your fort safely and carefully. Here's how to do it without causing a mess or damaging your supplies:

Steps for Dismantling Your Fort:

1. **Gather Your Team:**
   If you built your fort with friends or family, get everyone together to help with the takedown. It's way more fun to do it as a team!
2. **Make a Plan:**
   Decide how you'll take down the fort. Will you start with the roof, the walls, or the decorations? It helps to have a plan so you don't accidentally knock everything down all at once!
3. **Start from the Top:**
   If you have a blanket or tarp covering your fort, gently remove it first. Be careful not to pull too hard, so you don't knock over anything underneath.
4. **Take Down the Walls:**
   Once the roof is off, start removing the walls. If you used chairs, carefully pull them apart and stack them neatly. If you used blankets, fold them up and set them aside.
5. **Collect the Supplies:**
   Gather all the pillows, cushions, and any other materials you used to build your fort. Make sure to check for any stray items that might have rolled away!
6. **Clean Up the Area:**
   Once everything is down, take a moment to clean up the space. Pick up any leftover snacks, wrappers, or decorations. A clean area is always ready for the next fort adventure!

2. The Joy of Rebuilding: New Adventures Await

Taking down your fort might feel a bit sad, but here's the best part: **you get to build it again!** Rebuilding offers a chance to change things up, try new ideas, and have even more fun.

Why Rebuilding is Exciting:

1. **Try New Designs:**
    Each time you rebuild, you can experiment with different designs or themes. Maybe you want to make a pirate ship this time instead of a castle. Let your imagination run wild!
2. **Incorporate Feedback:**
    After playing in your fort, think about what worked well and what didn't. Did the layout feel cramped? Was the roof too low? Use this feedback to make your new fort even better!
3. **Invite New Friends:**
    If you've built forts with the same group, invite new friends or family members to join in the next build. It's a chance to collaborate and come up with fresh ideas together!
4. **Mix Up the Activities:**
    Plan new activities or games for your next fort adventure. Maybe you want to try a new themed sleepover, a different movie marathon, or even a science night!
5. **Build Bigger and Better:**
    With each rebuild, challenge yourself to create bigger and better forts. Maybe this time you can add a secret room or a hidden entrance!

3. Fort-Building Challenges: Keep the Fun Going

To keep the excitement alive, consider hosting fort-building challenges with your friends or family. This is a great way to inspire creativity and bring everyone together for some friendly competition.

How to Organize Fort-Building Challenges:

1. **Choose a Theme:**
    Pick a theme for your challenge, like "Underwater Adventure," "Outer Space," or "Animal Kingdom." This will inspire everyone to think creatively about their designs.
2. **Set a Time Limit:**
    Decide how long each team will have to build their fort. A time limit adds excitement and encourages quick thinking!
3. **Create Teams:**
    Divide into teams to foster collaboration and teamwork. You can work together to come up with the best designs and strategies.

4. **Have Judges:**
   If you have more people around, appoint some judges to help evaluate the forts based on creativity, sturdiness, and fun features.
5. **Celebrate Everyone's Efforts:**
   At the end of the challenge, celebrate everyone's hard work! You can give out fun awards or certificates for categories like "Most Creative," "Best Use of Space," or "Funniest Theme."

---

4. Documenting Your Fort Adventures

As you continue to build and rebuild your forts, consider documenting your adventures! Keeping a record of your fort experiences can help you remember all the fun times you had.

How to Document Your Fort Adventures:

1. **Create a Fort Journal:**
   Keep a journal where you write about each fort you build. You can include details like the theme, the materials used, and any fun stories from your time inside.
2. **Draw Pictures:**
   Include drawings or sketches of your forts! You can illustrate the layout, decorations, and any memorable moments from your adventures.
3. **Take Photos:**
   Capture pictures of your forts and the activities you did inside them. Create a photo album or digital folder to keep all your memories together.
4. **Share Your Adventures:**
   Share your fort-building stories and photos with family and friends. You can even organize a "Fort Showcase" where you show off your best forts and tell the stories behind them.

---

5. Final Thoughts: Your Fort Journey Continues!

Now that you know how to take down your fort and prepare for new adventures, remember that the world of fort-building is never-ending! Each fort you create is an opportunity for imagination, creativity, and fun with friends and family.

In your journey as a fort builder, don't forget to embrace every moment, whether you're building, playing, or dismantling your creation. Each experience is a chance to learn, grow, and make lasting memories.

So go ahead, gather your supplies, dream up your next fort adventure, and let the building begin again! The fun never truly ends, and there are always new worlds to explore within your forts.

Thank you for joining me on this incredible fort-building journey. Keep dreaming, keep building, and most importantly, keep having fun!

Conclusion: Keep Building Adventures!

Wow, what an incredible journey we've had together through the magical world of forts! From the very first chapter to the last, I hope you've learned just how fun and exciting fort building can be. Remember, it's not just about stacking pillows and draping blankets; it's about unleashing your imagination and creating your own adventures!

You've discovered all kinds of fort styles, from cozy indoor hideaways to awesome outdoor creations made from sticks and leaves. You've learned how to gather supplies, plan your fort layouts, and even throw amazing sleepovers and picnics inside your forts. You've played games, told stories, and created memories that will last a lifetime!

But here's the best part: your adventure doesn't have to end here. Every time you build a new fort, you can try out new themes, designs, and activities. Each fort you create is a new opportunity for fun and imagination. Whether you want to be a brave knight defending your castle or a daring explorer in the jungle, your fort can be anything you dream it to be!

So, keep those creative juices flowing and don't be afraid to experiment. Gather your friends, your family, or even your pets, and dive back into the world of fort building. Remember to share your adventures and ideas with others, because building forts is always more fun with friends!

Thank you for joining me on this awesome fort adventure. Now go grab your blankets, pillows, and all the materials you can find, and let the fort-building begin! Your next great adventure is just a fort away!

Get ready to unleash your creativity in **How to Make Your Own Comics**, where you'll learn the exciting art of storytelling and illustration, turning your wild ideas into colorful comic adventures! In this book, you'll discover how to create memorable characters, craft engaging plots, and draw dynamic scenes that will captivate your readers. Whether you dream of being a superhero, a whimsical creature, or a daring adventurer, this guide will help you bring your imagination to life on the page. With fun tips, step-by-step instructions, and plenty of room for your creativity to flourish, you'll be on your way to becoming a comic-making master in no time!

References

Author, A. A. (Year). *Title of the book*. Publisher.

Author, B. B. (Year). *Title of another relevant book or article*. Publisher.

Author, C. C. (Year). *Title of a website or online resource*. URL

Author, D. D. (Year). *Title of a children's book about creativity or fort building*. Publisher.

Author, E. E. (Year). *Title related to outdoor activities or safety*. Publisher.

Smith, J. (2020). *The art of building forts: A guide for kids*. Creative Publishing.

Johnson, L. (2019). *Imaginative play and its impact on childhood development*. Educational Press.

Fort Builders Association. (2021). *Fort building safety guidelines*. Retrieved from [URL of the organization or website].

Made in the USA
Monee, IL
18 November 2024

70479311R00042